Dear Parent:
Your child's love of reading starts here!

Every child learns to read in a different way and at his or her own speed. Some go back and forth between reading levels and read favorite books again and again. Others read through each level in order. You can help your young reader improve and become more confident by encouraging his or her own interests and abilities. From books your child reads with you to the first books he or she reads alone, there are I Can Read Books for every stage of reading:

SHARED READING
Basic language, word repetition, and whimsical illustrations, ideal for sharing with your emergent reader

BEGINNING READING
Short sentences, familiar words, and simple concepts for children eager to read on their own

READING WITH HELP
Engaging stories, longer sentences, and language play for developing readers

READING ALONE
Complex plots, challenging vocabulary, and high-interest topics for the independent reader

ADVANCED READING
Short paragraphs, chapters, and exciting ther̶ for the perfect bridge to chapter books

I Can Read Books have introduced children to t̶ since 1957. Featuring award-winning authors and illust̶r̶a̶c̶ fabulous cast of beloved characters, I Can Read Books set the standard for beginning readers.

A lifetime of discovery begins with the magical words "I Can Read!"

Visit www.icanread.com for information
on enriching your child's reading experience.

I Can Read Book® is a trademark of HarperCollins Publishers.

Wonder Woman: Maze of Magic
Copyright © 2017 DC Comics.
WONDER WOMAN and all related characters and elements © & ™ DC Comics.
(s17)

HARP38035
Manufactured in U.S.A. No part of this book may be used or reproduced in any manner whatsoever
without written permission except in the case of brief quotations embodied in critical articles and reviews.
For information address HarperCollins Children's Books, a division of HarperCollins Publishers,
195 Broadway, New York, NY 10007.
www.icanread.com

ISBN 978-0-06-236093-9

Book design by Erica De Chavez
17 18 19 20 21 LSCC 10 9 8 7 6 5 4 3 2
❖
First Edition

I Can Read!™
READING 2 WITH HELP

WONDER WOMAN™

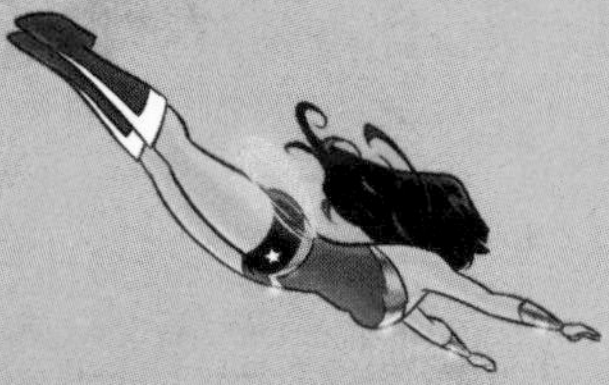

MAZE OF MAGIC

story by Liz Marsham
pictures by Lee Ferguson

Wonder Woman created by
William Moulton Marston

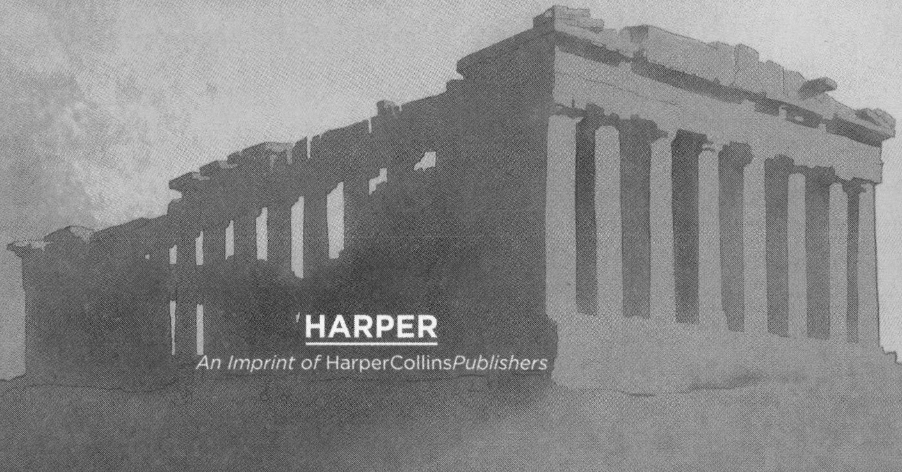

HARPER
An Imprint of HarperCollinsPublishers

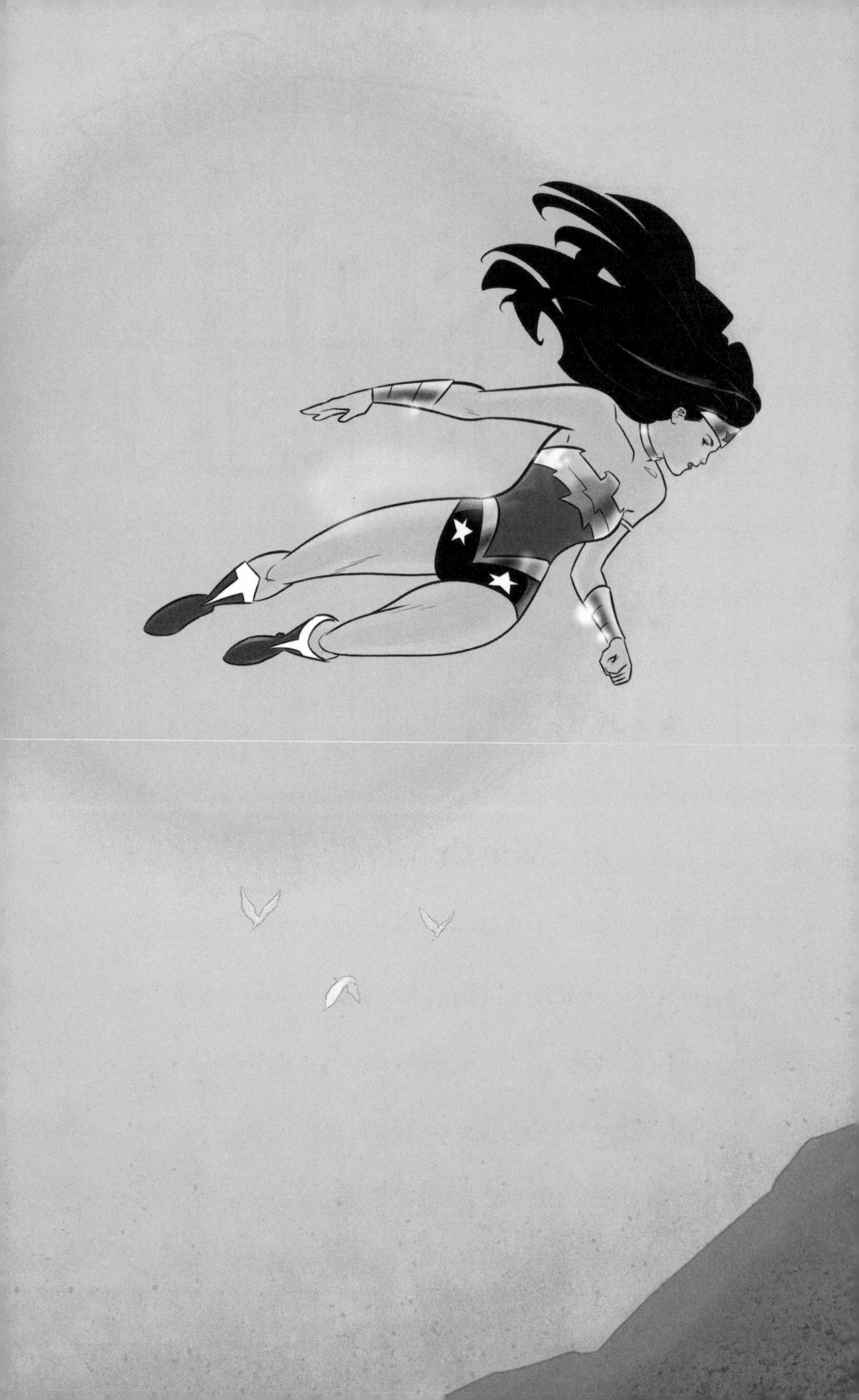

Wonder Woman soared over
the land, searching for
a missing family.
The family had gone for a hike
the day before.
When they didn't return,
Wonder Woman was called in
to help find them.

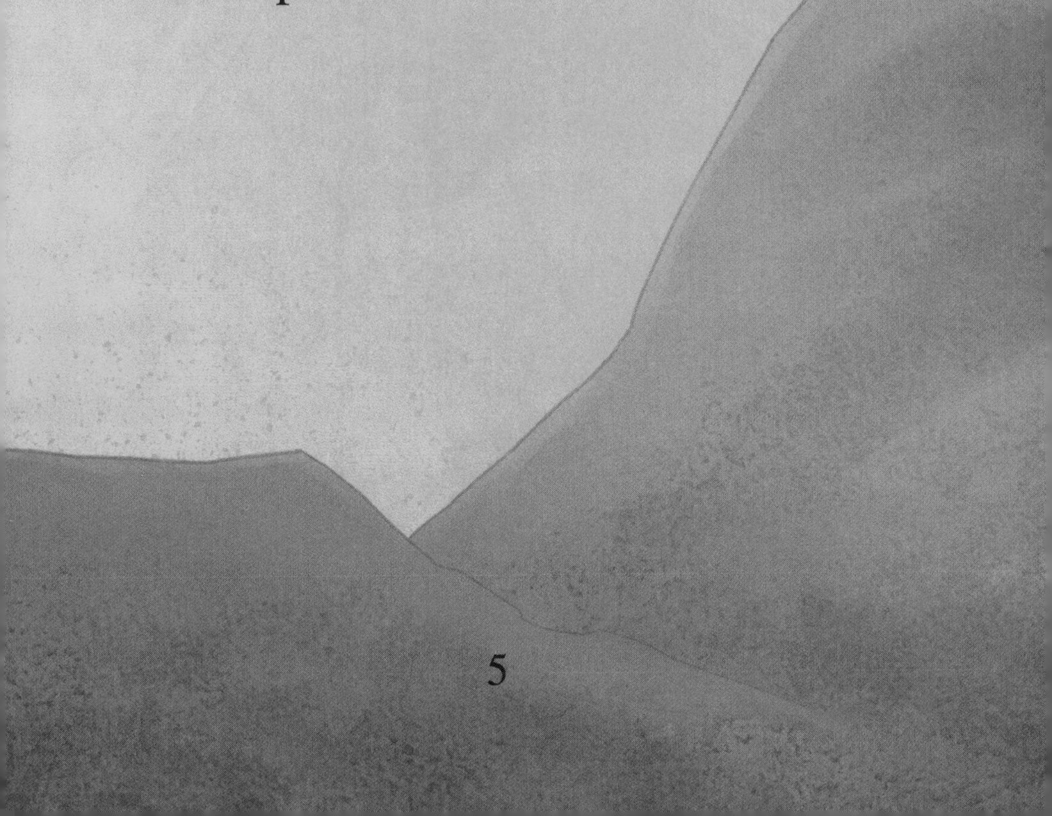

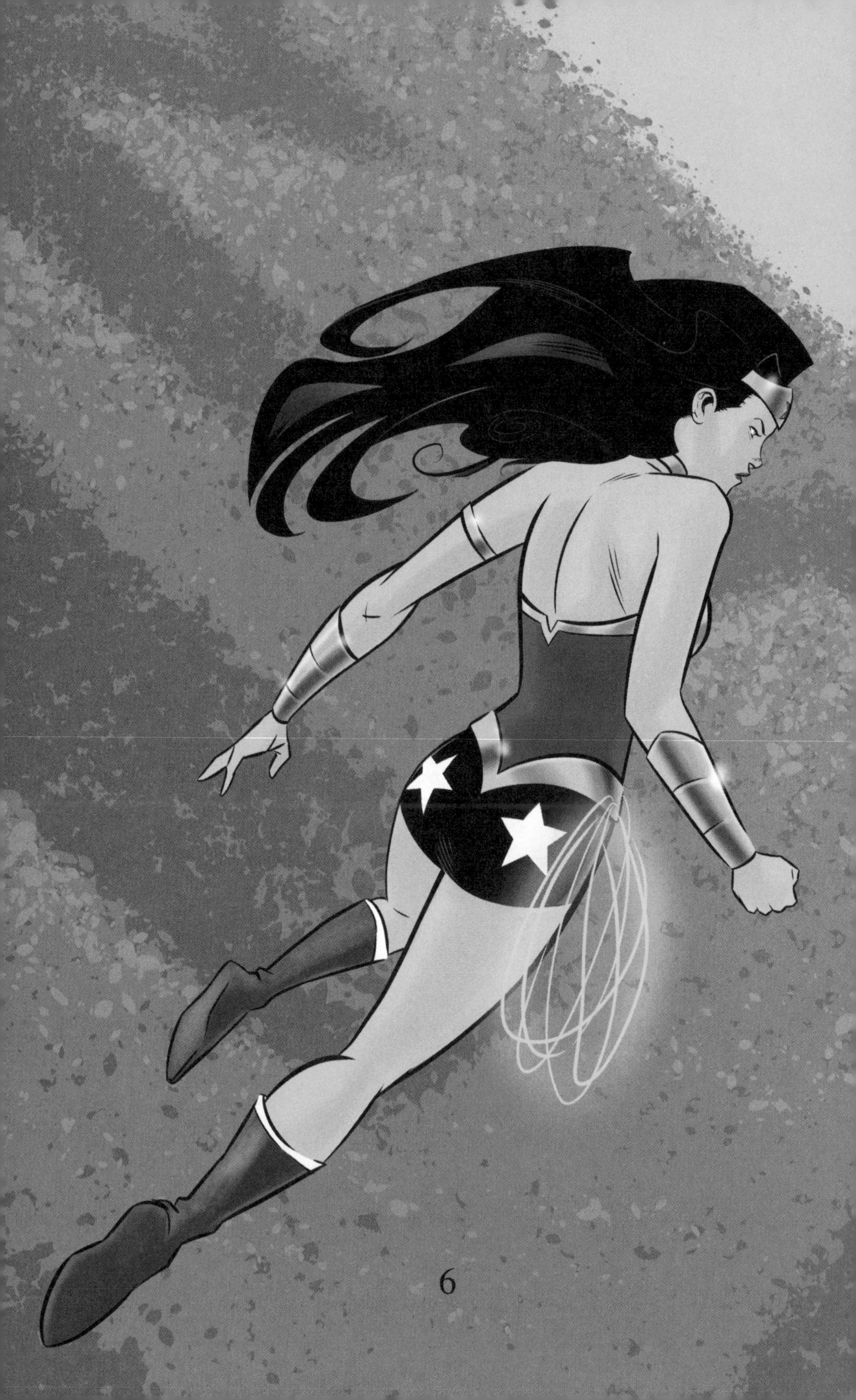

From the air, Wonder Woman
spotted a hidden valley.
The valley was covered
by a huge maze made of plants.
She flew down to investigate.

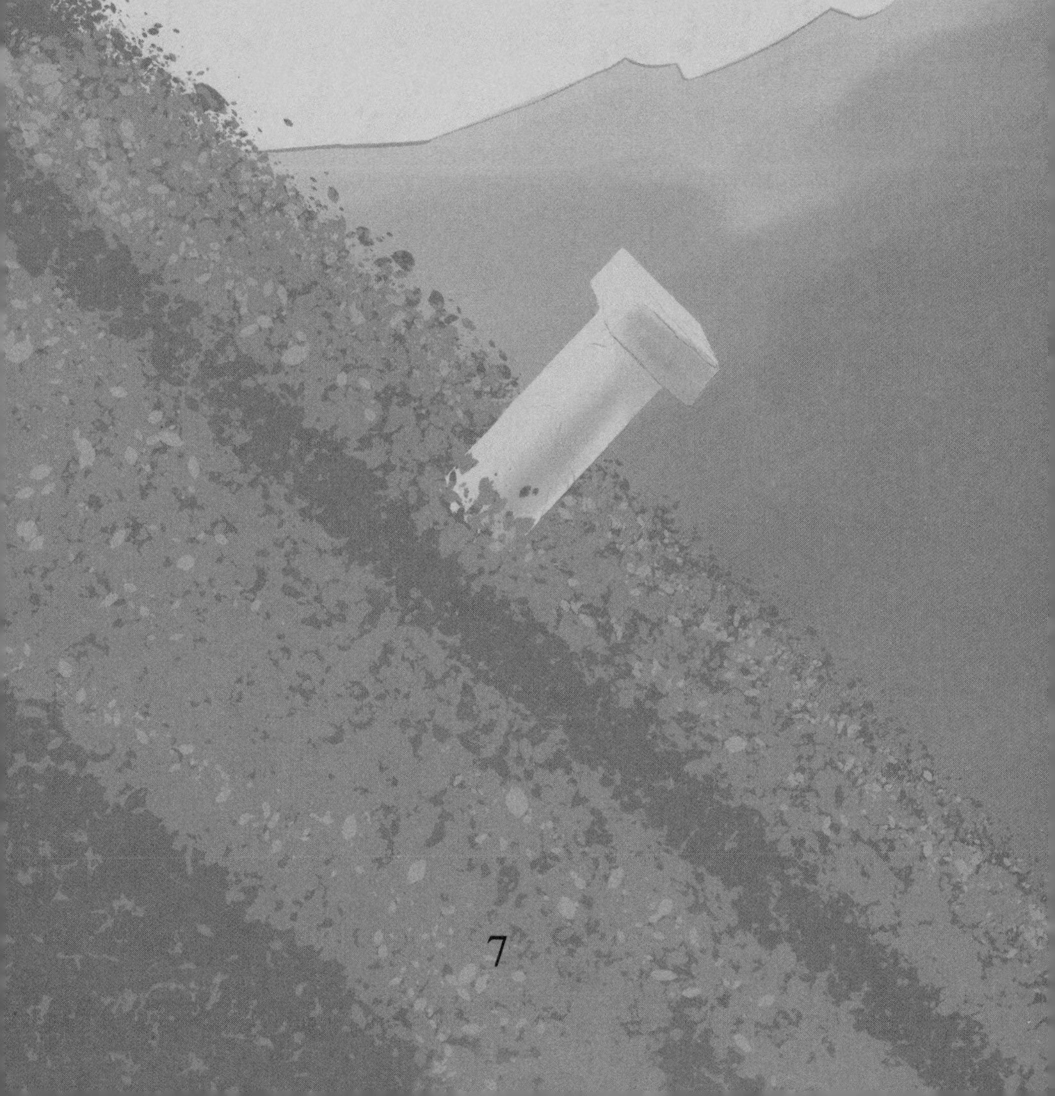

Wonder Woman entered the maze.
She discovered something
very strange.
Animals filled the maze.

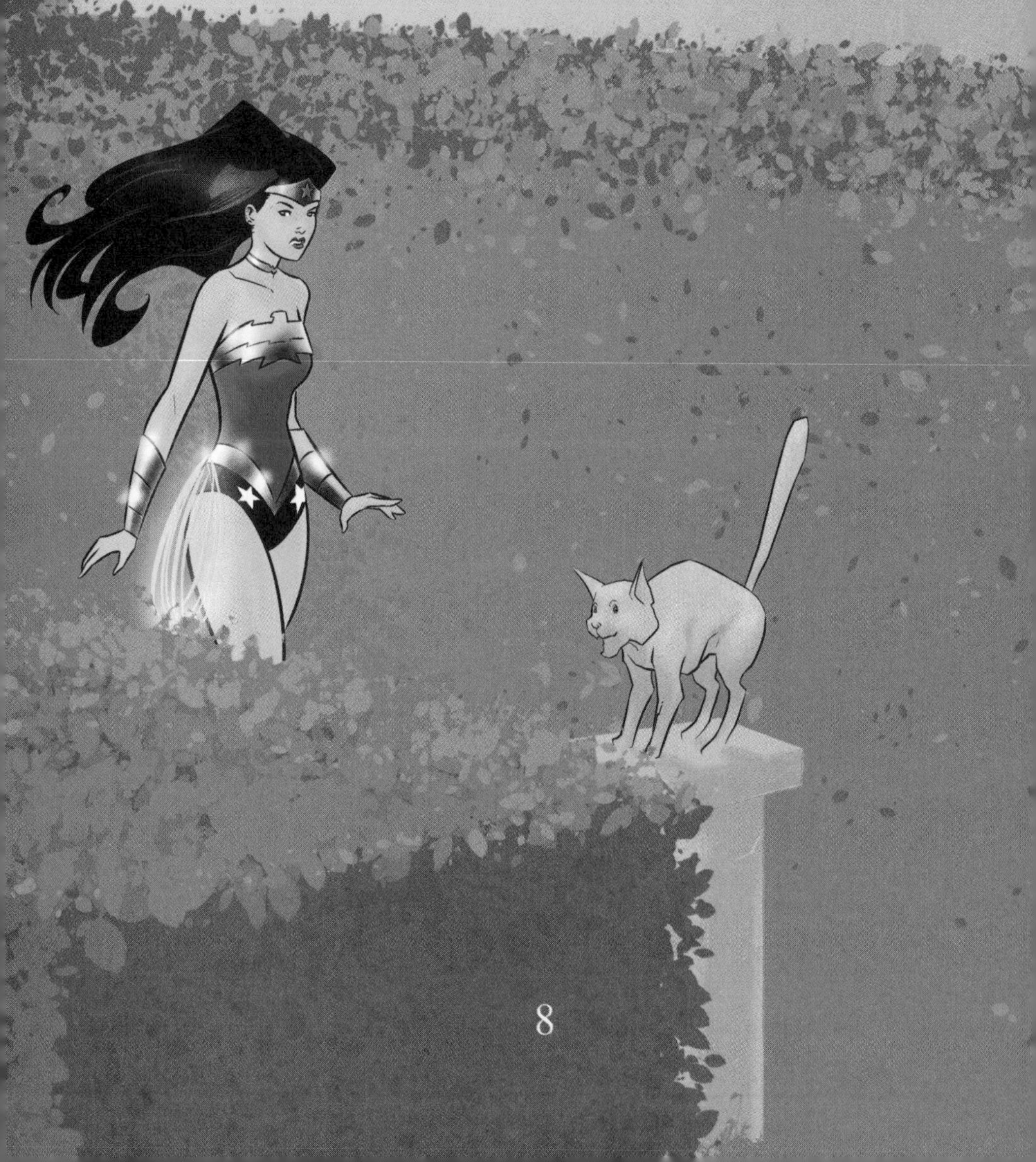

She took a closer look.
The animals were statues,
but they looked real.

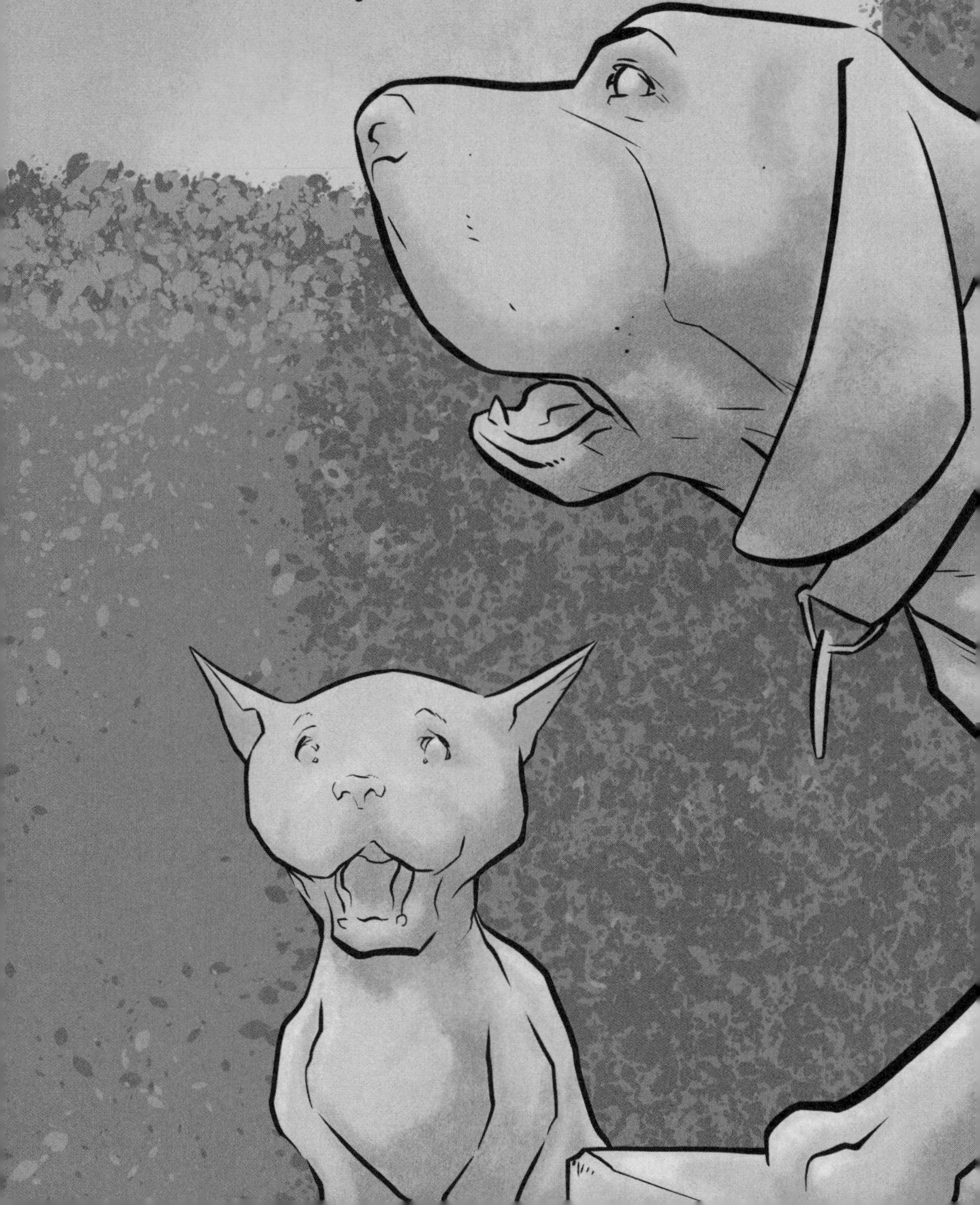

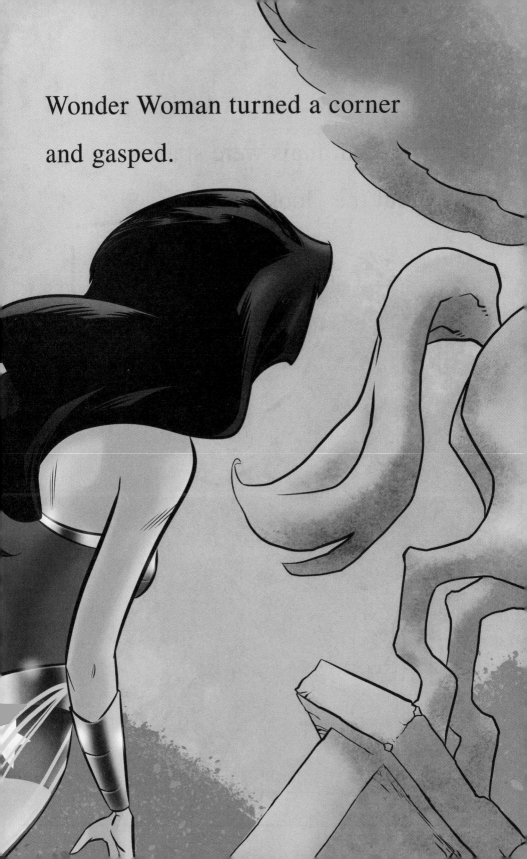

Wonder Woman turned a corner and gasped.

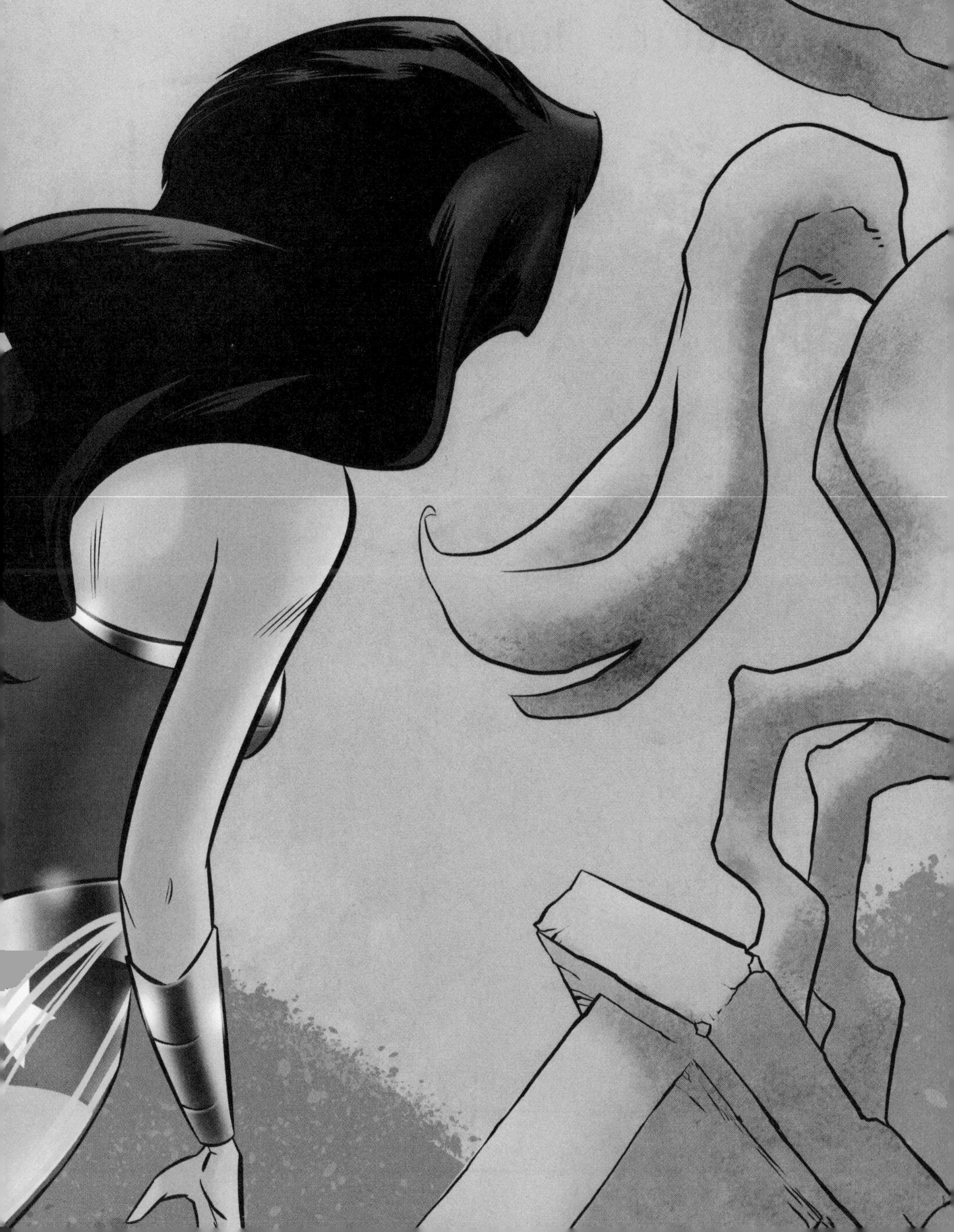

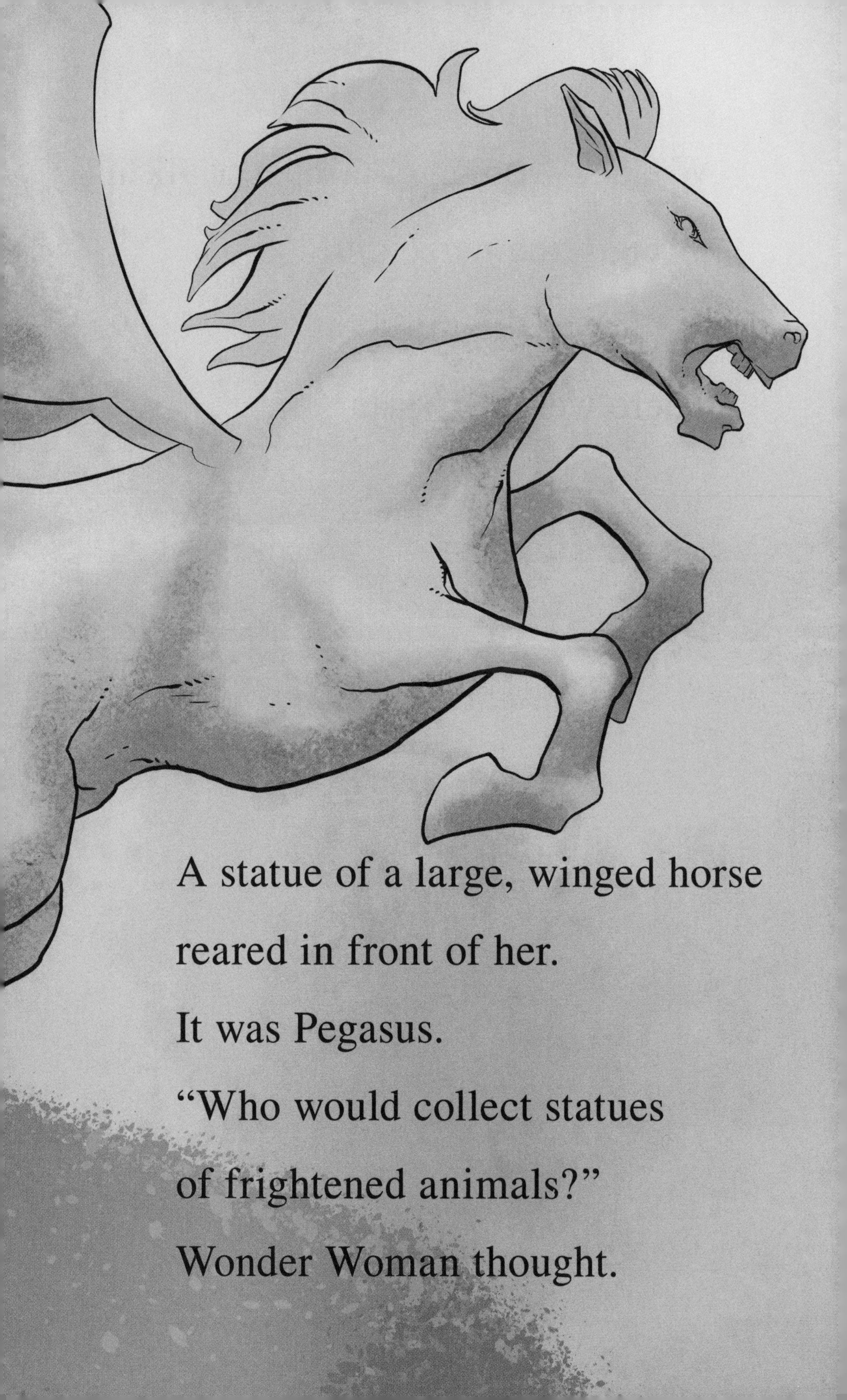

A statue of a large, winged horse
reared in front of her.
It was Pegasus.
"Who would collect statues
of frightened animals?"
Wonder Woman thought.

Wonder Woman continued walking
through the maze until
she found the middle.
There were three statues.

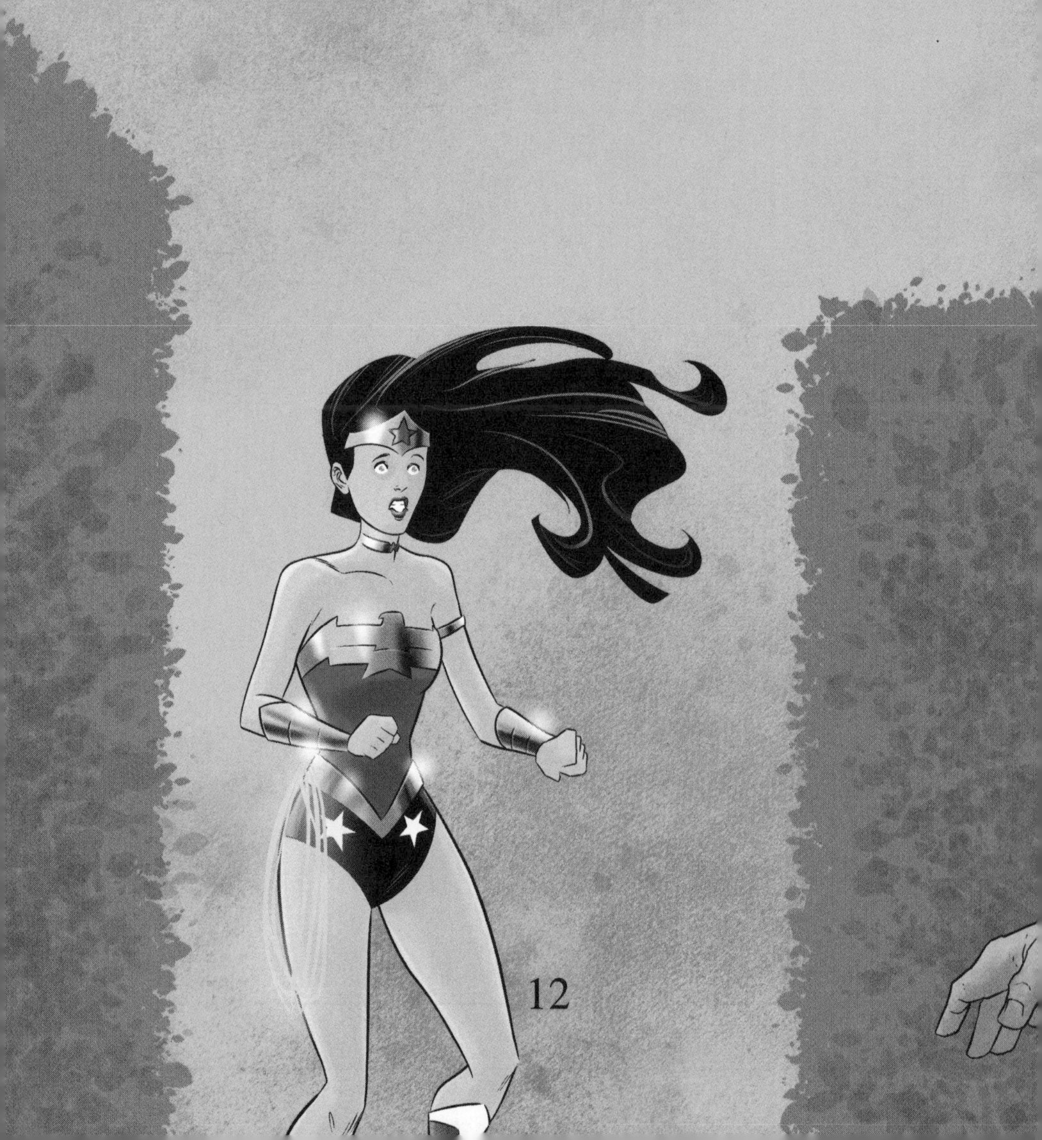

She looked more closely.

The statues looked familiar.

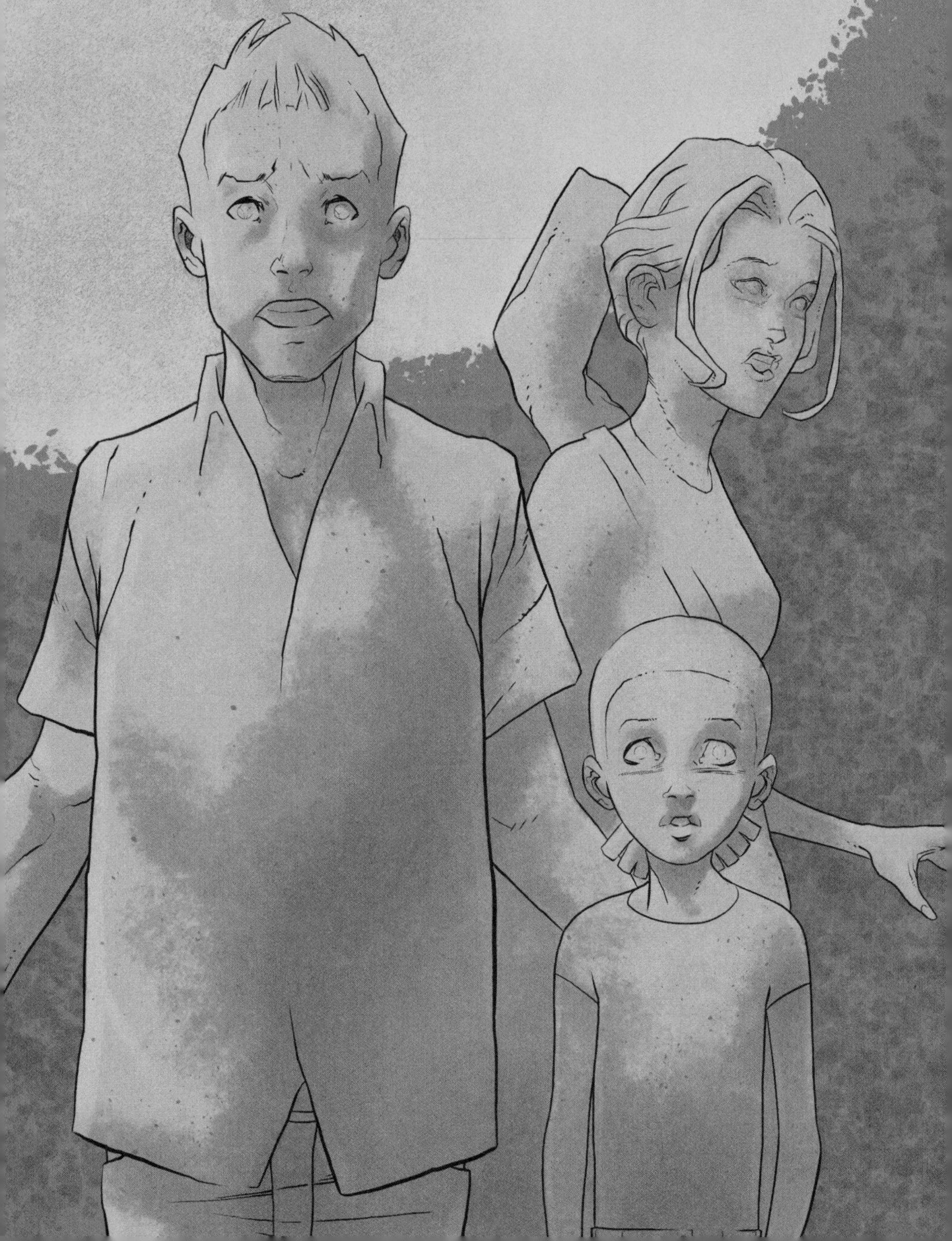

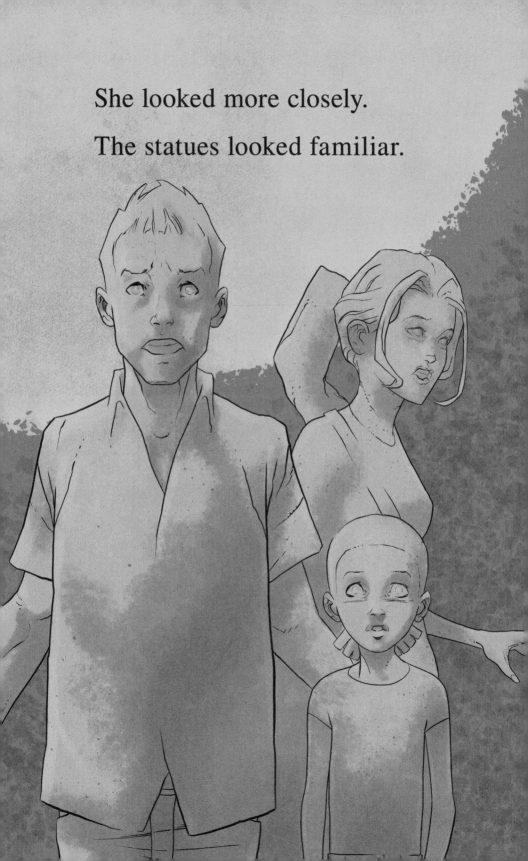

Wonder Woman continued
to examine the statues.
"These look like
the missing family," she said.
"Someone is turning living things
into stone!"

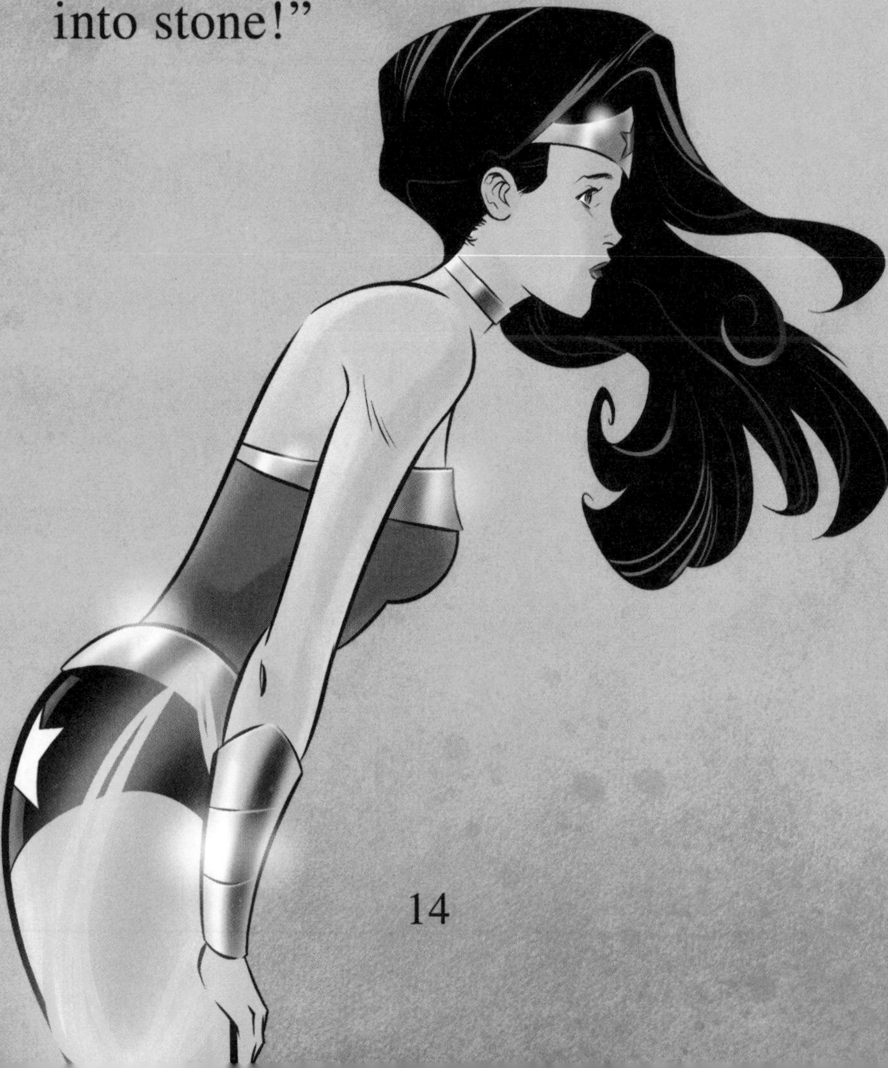

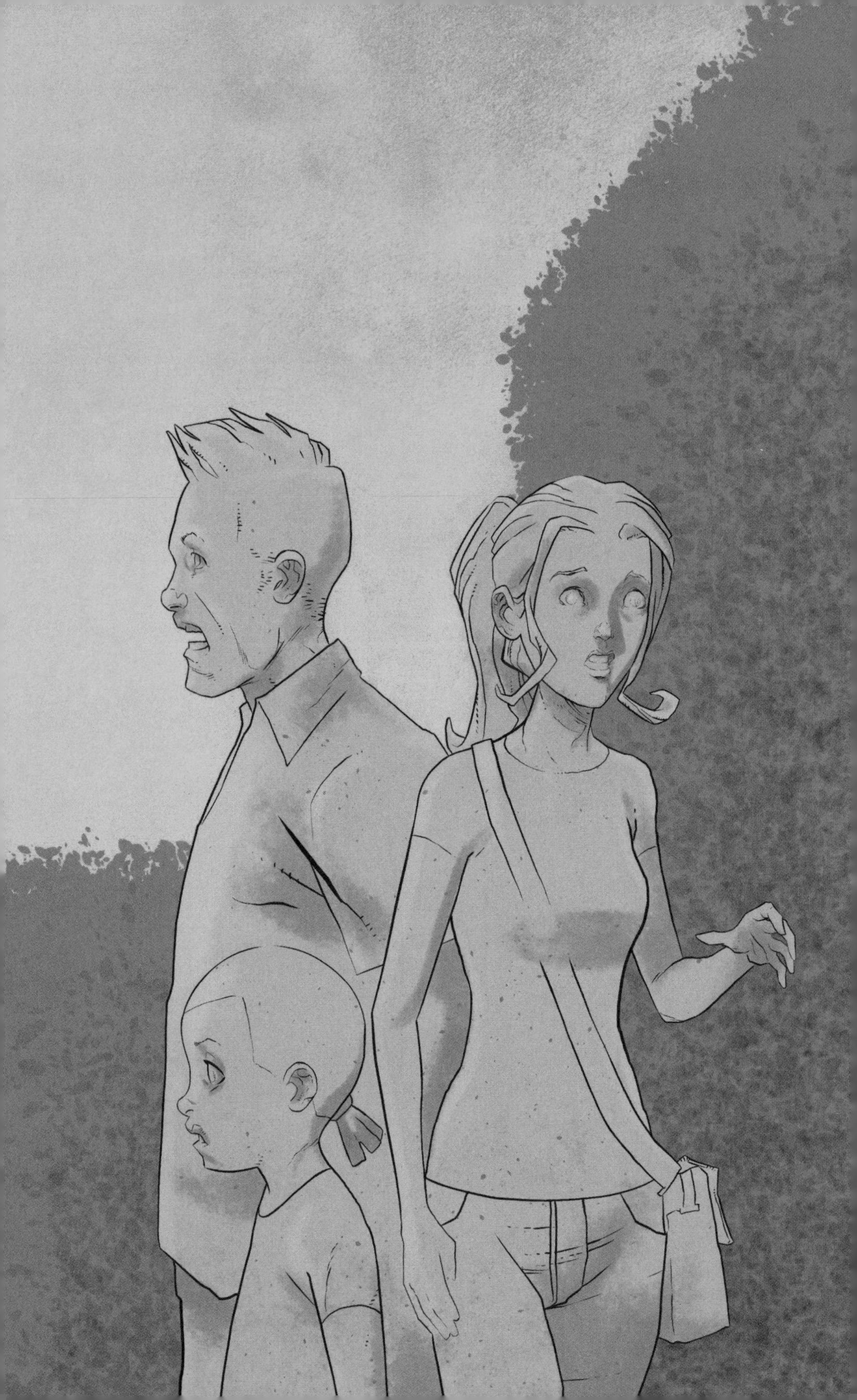

Wonder Woman heard footsteps
behind her.
Someone was coming
through the maze!

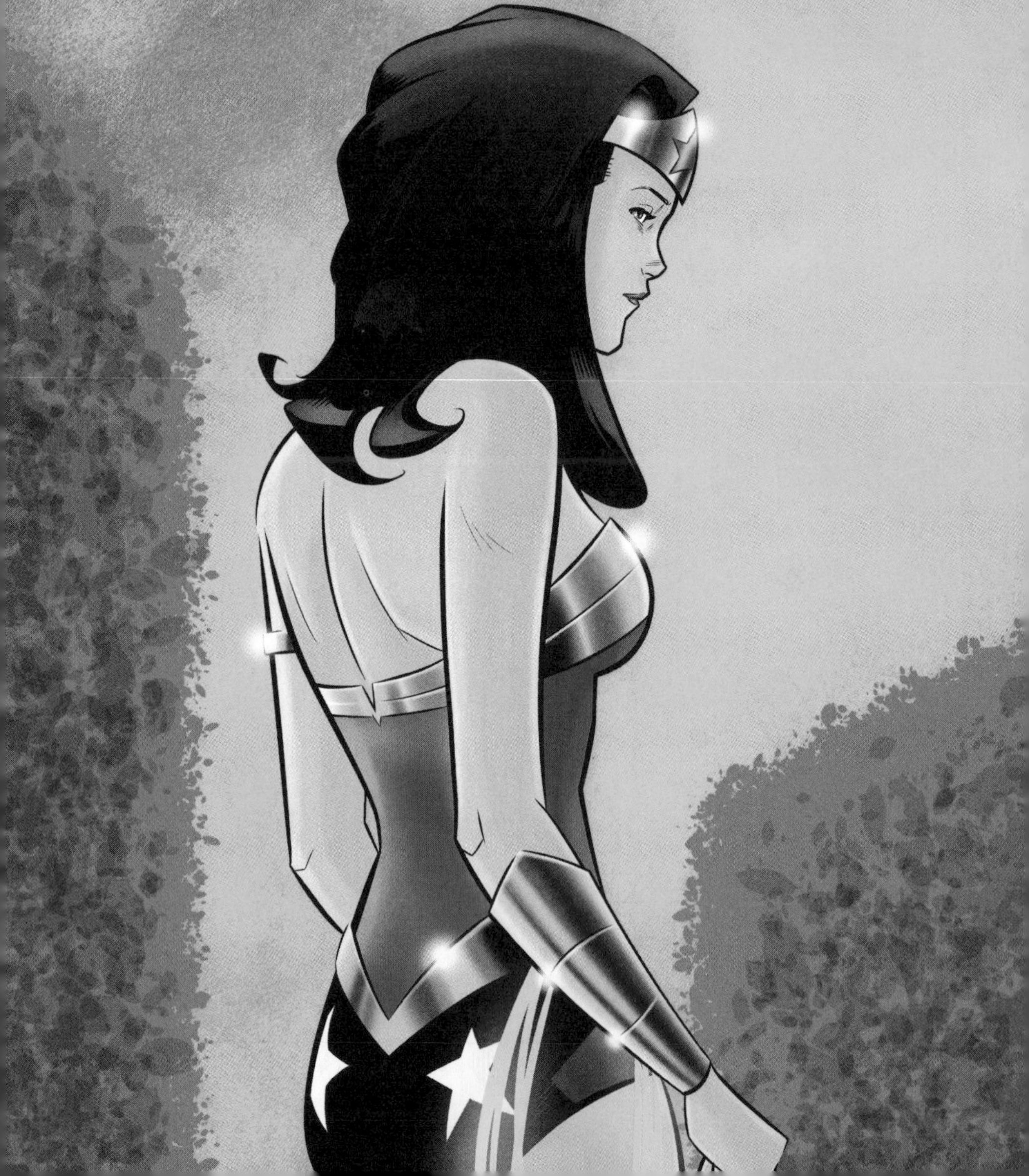

Wonder Woman heard

a strange hissing noise.

"Snakes!" said Wonder Woman.

"It must be Medusa!"

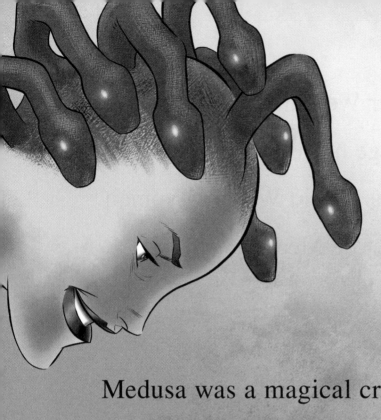

Medusa was a magical creature
called a gorgon.

She had snakes for hair.

Anyone who looked at her

turned to stone.

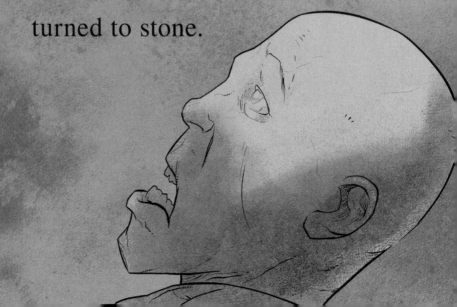

Medusa rushed into
the center of the maze.
There was nothing there
except the statues.

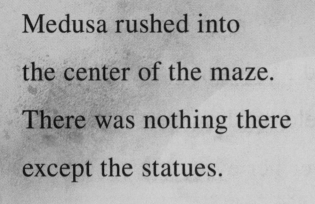

Wonder Woman landed quietly

behind Medusa.

She held her bracelets up

to cover her eyes.

Medusa turned to look.

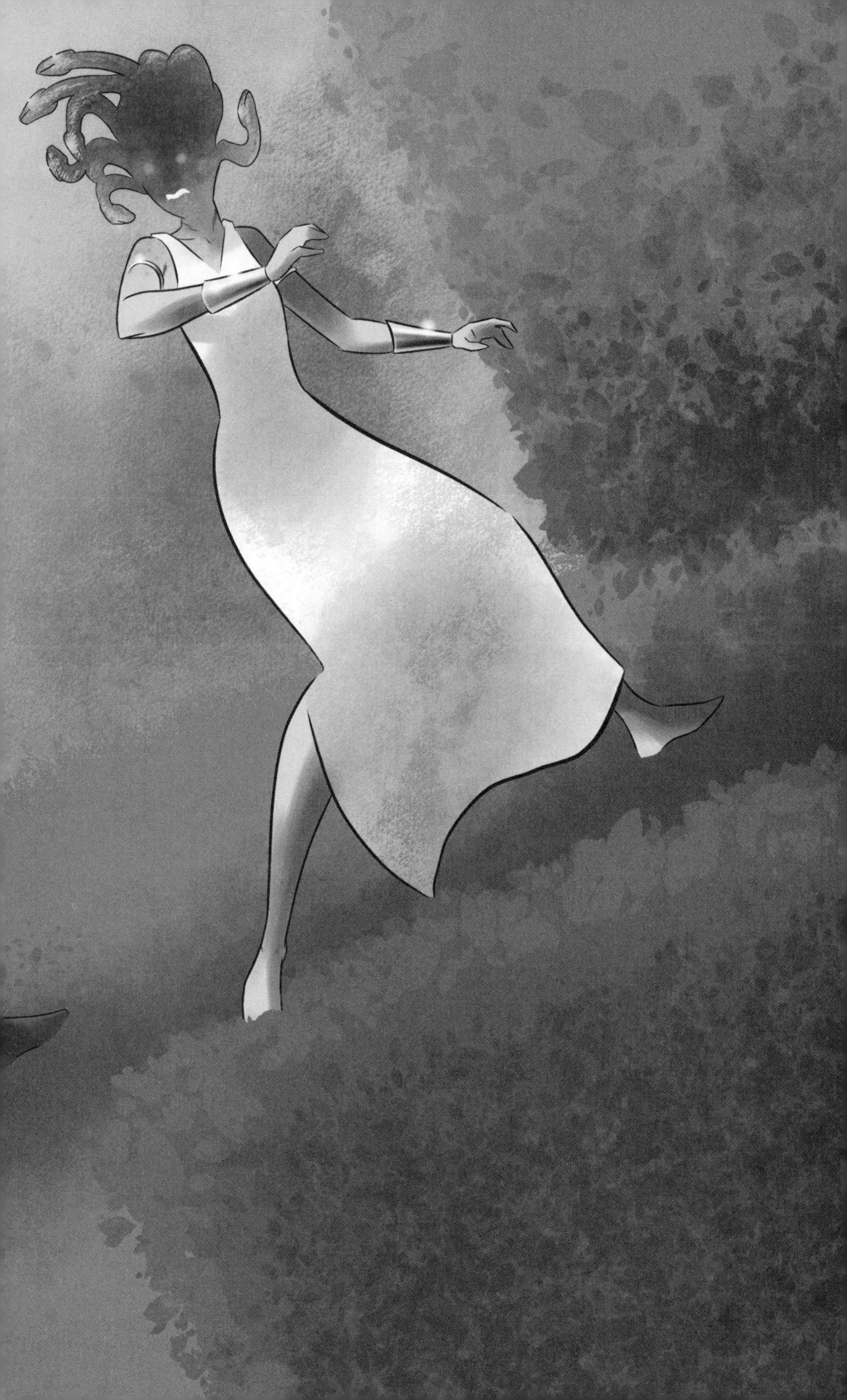

The shiny bracelets

were like mirrors.

Medusa saw her reflection in them.

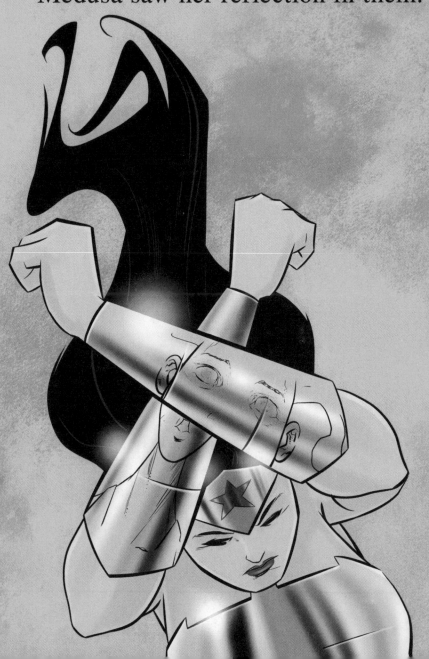

Medusa tried to look away,
but it was too late!
She turned to stone.

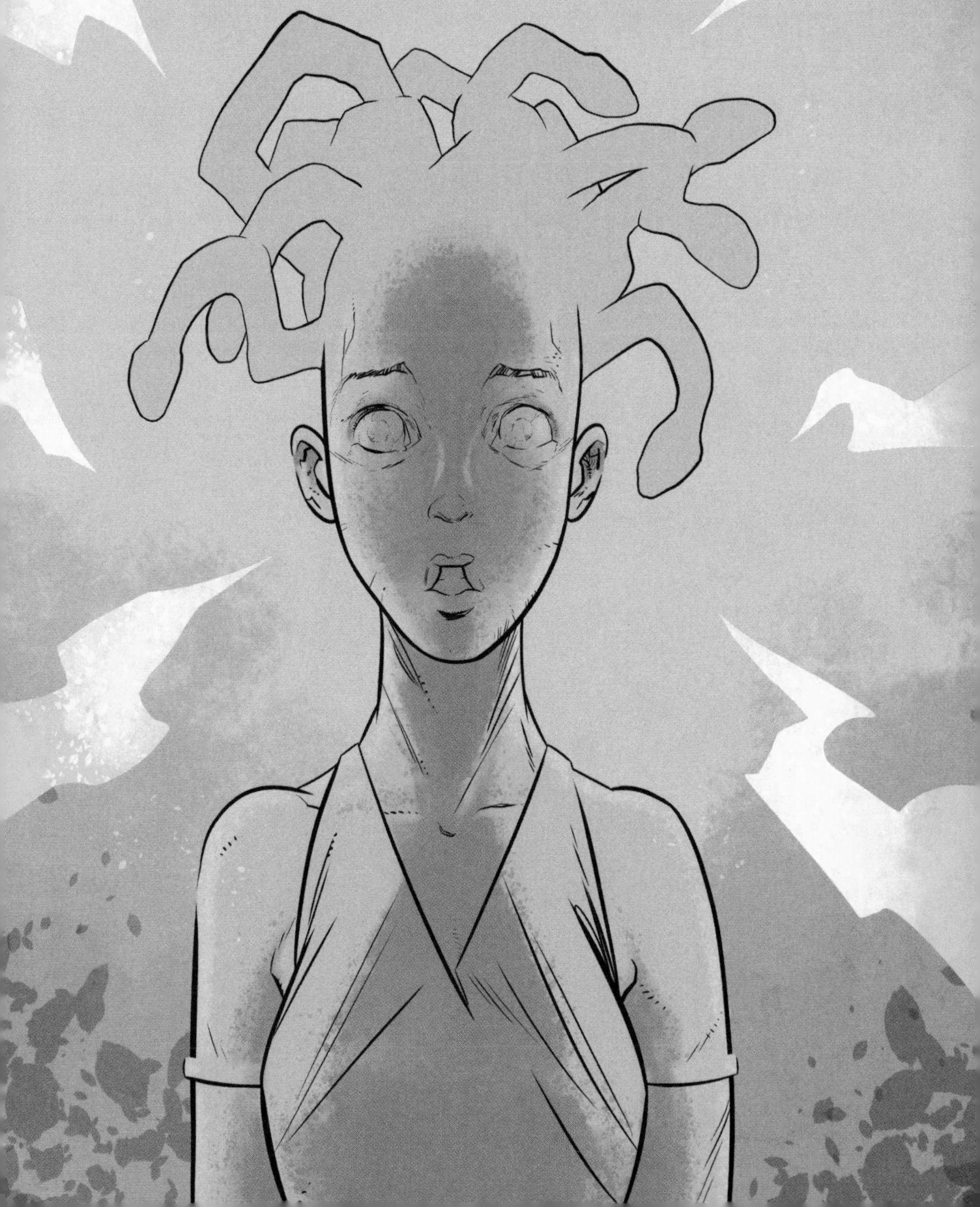

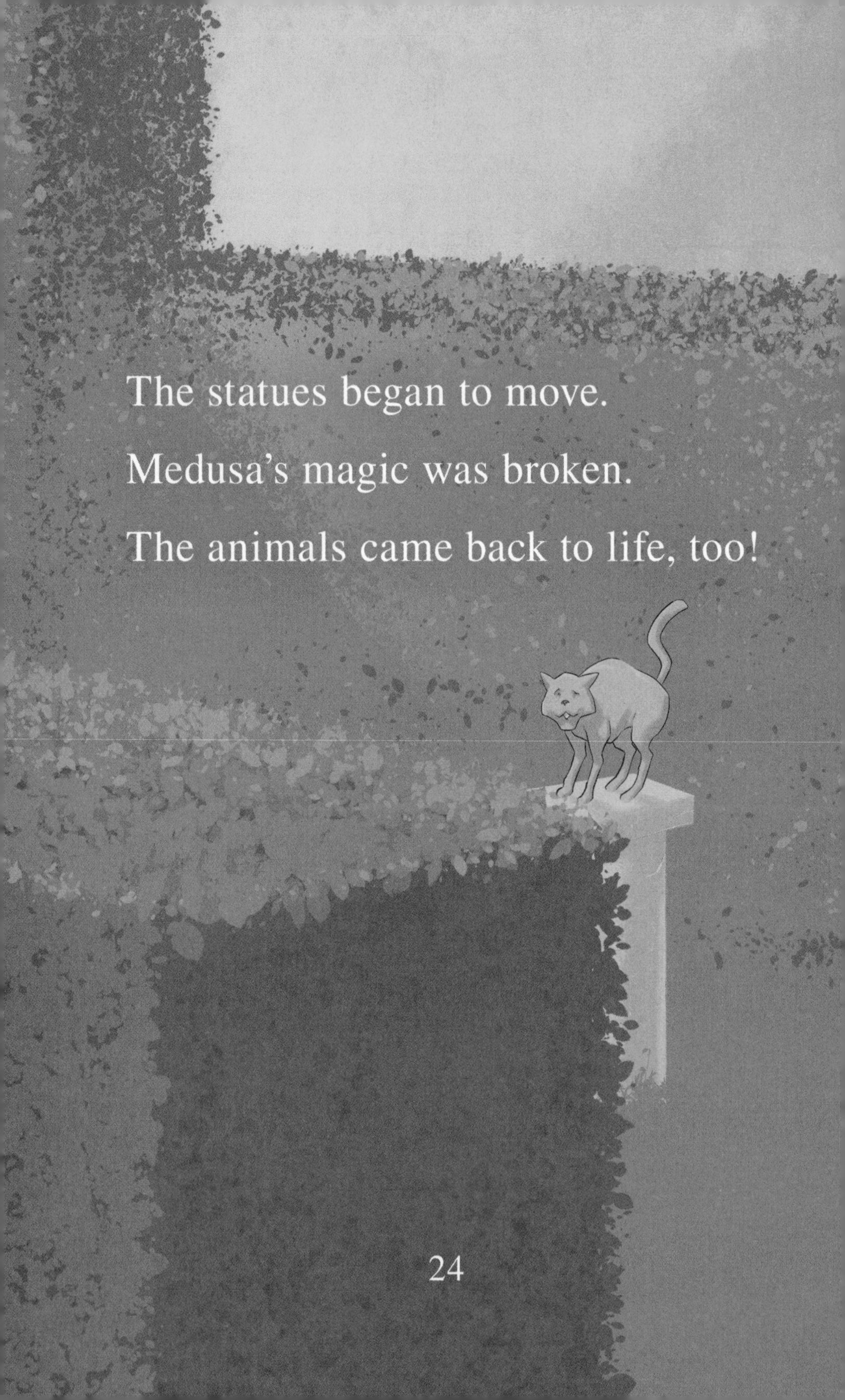

The statues began to move.

Medusa's magic was broken.

The animals came back to life, too!

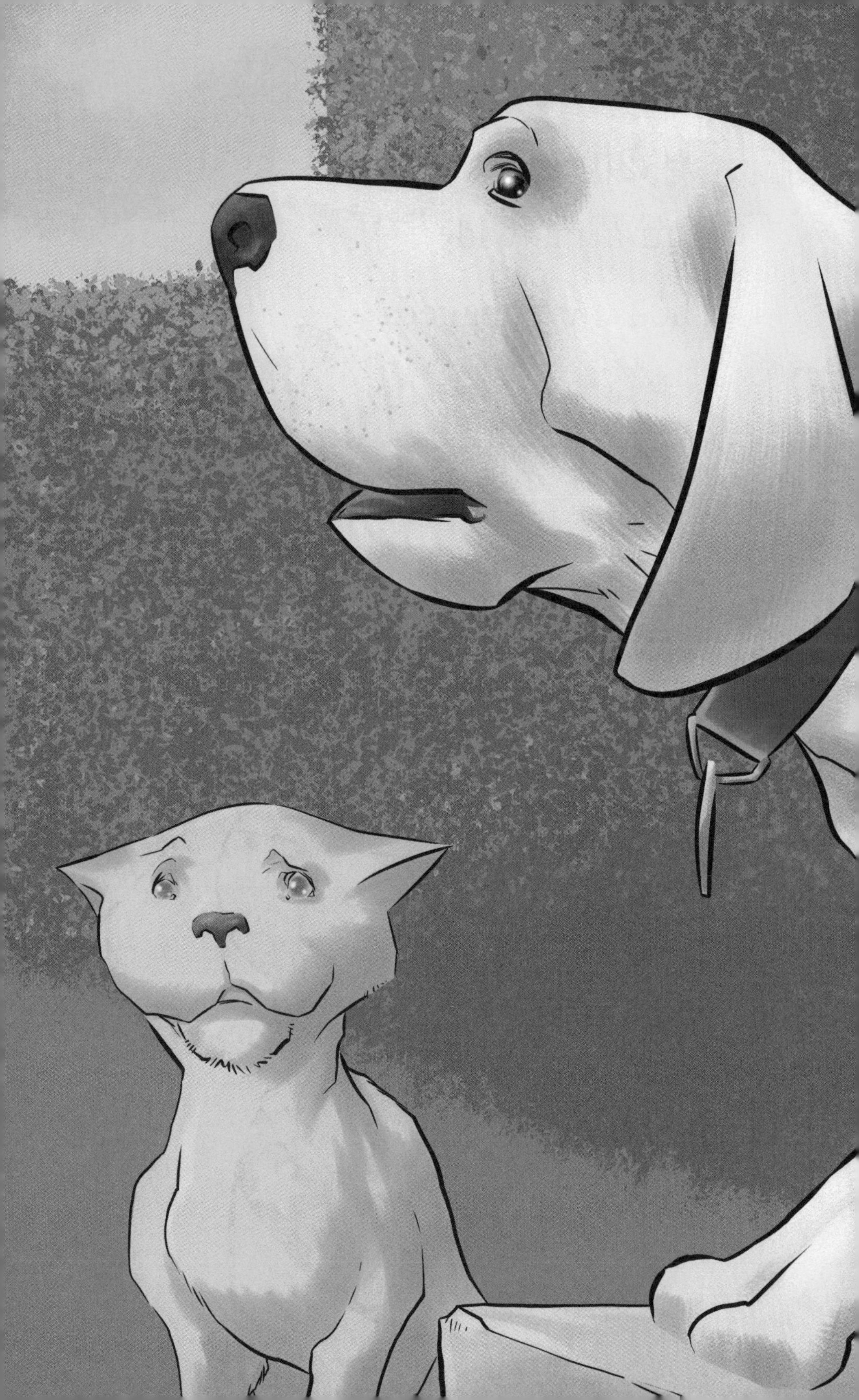

The girl and her parents stretched their arms wide.

Then they hugged.

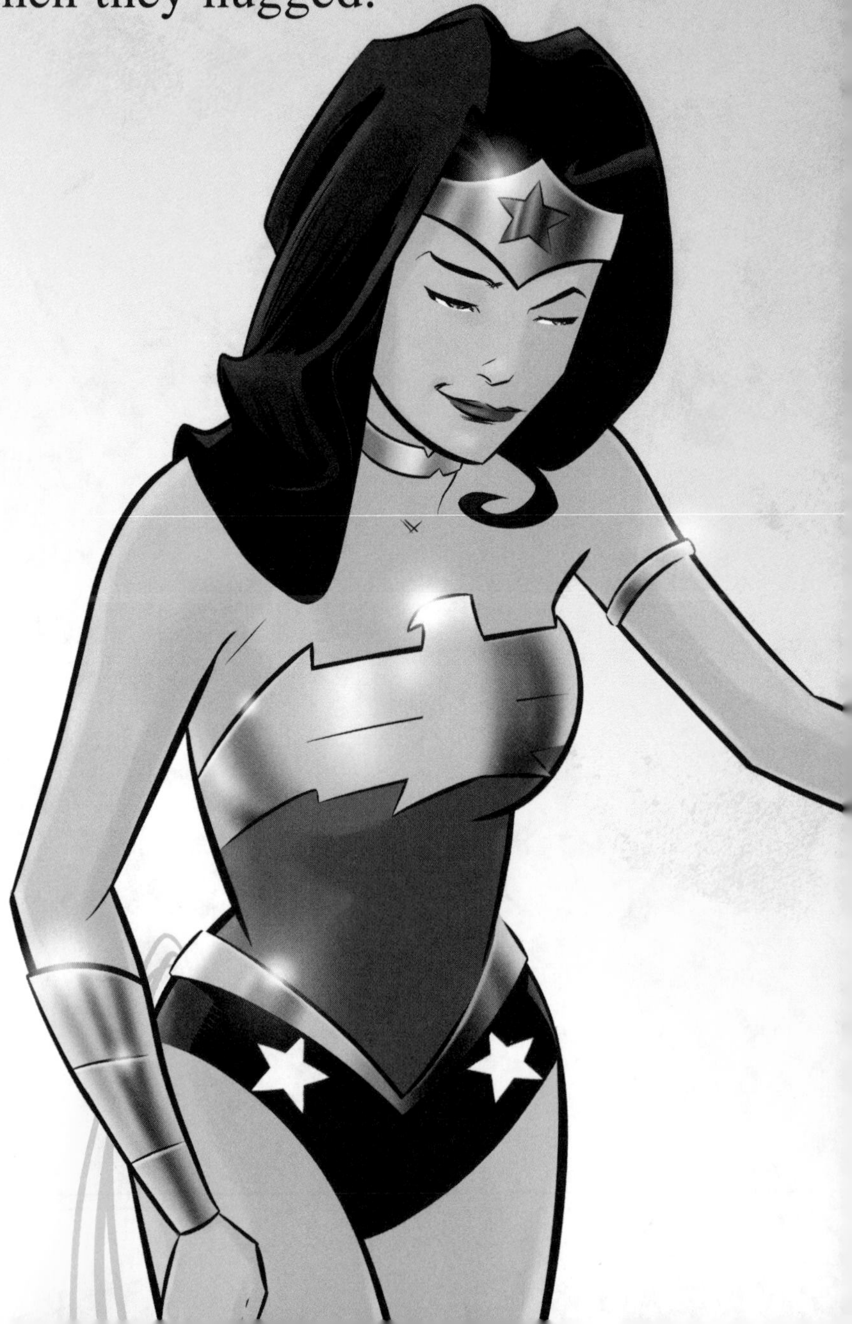

“Thank you for saving us,”
the girl said to Wonder Woman.

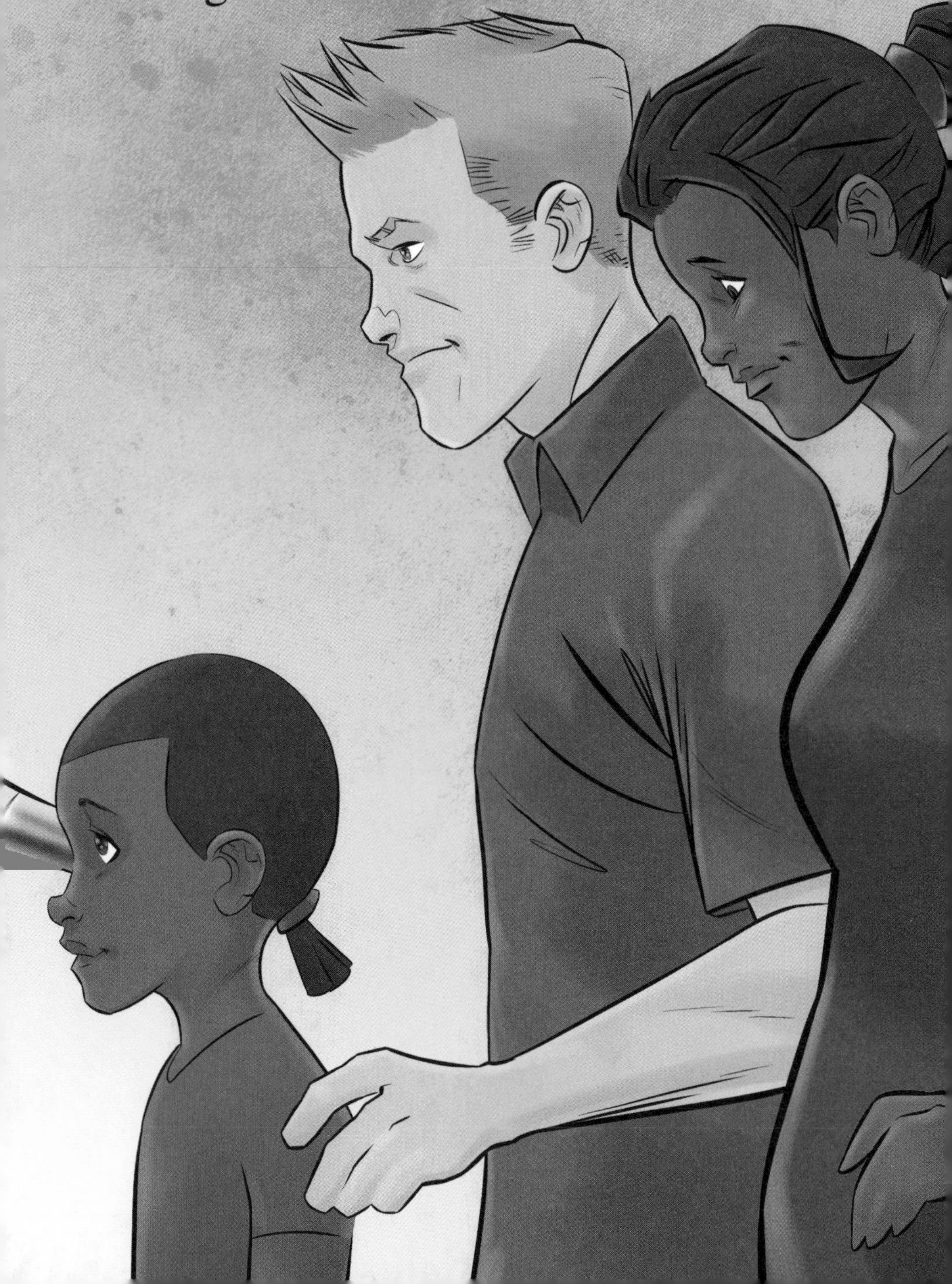

Pegasus trotted toward them.

The girl jumped up and down.

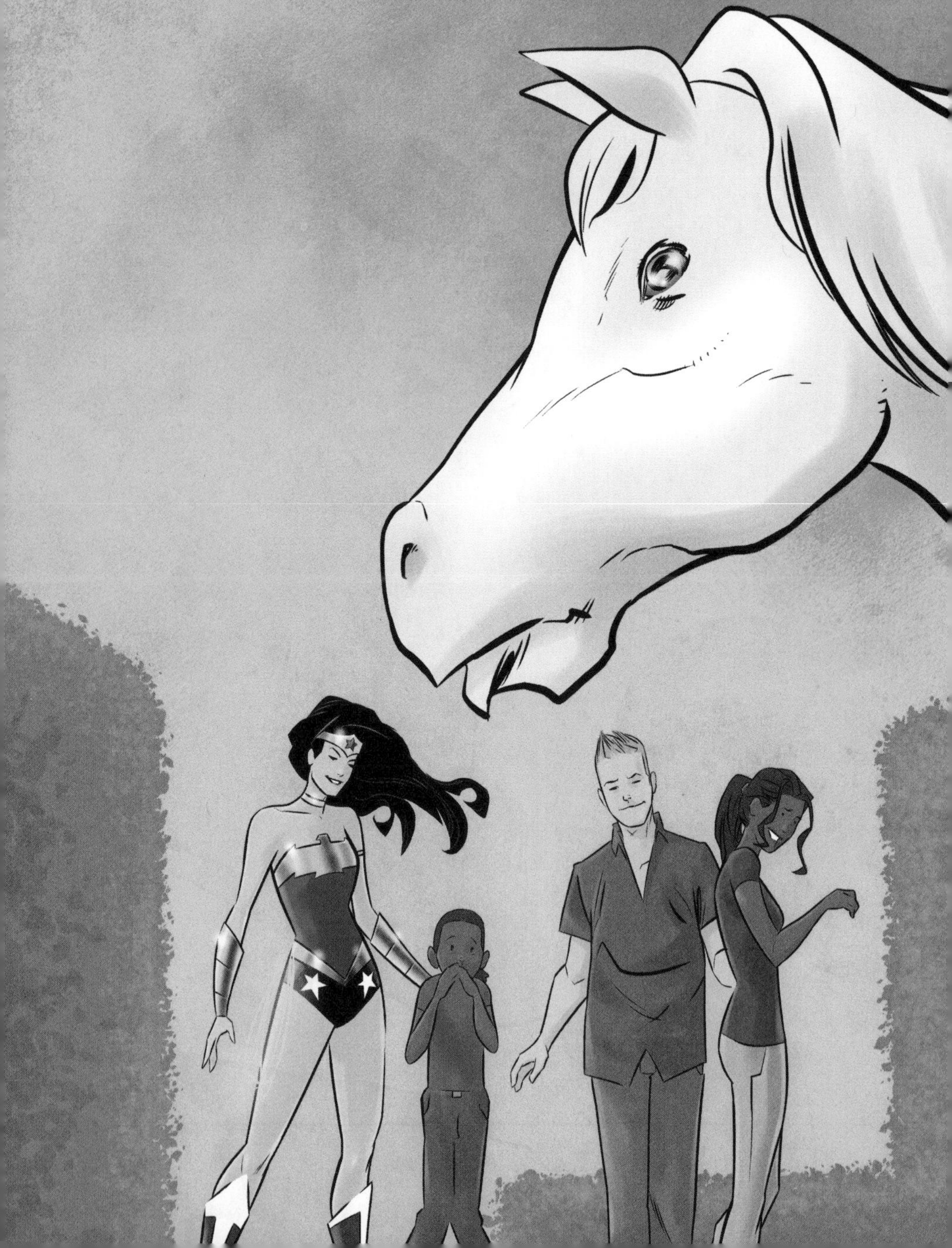

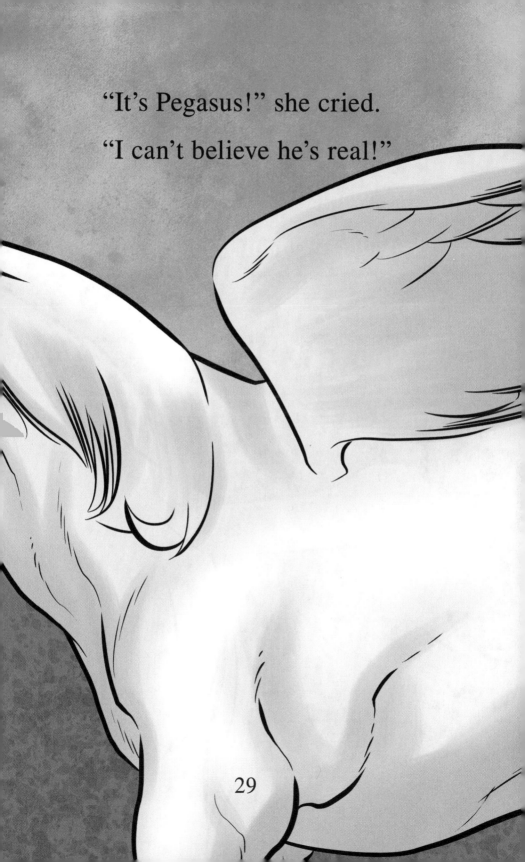

"It's Pegasus!" she cried.

"I can't believe he's real!"

29

Pegasus kneeled down
in front of the girl.
"He wants to give you a ride,"
Wonder Woman said.

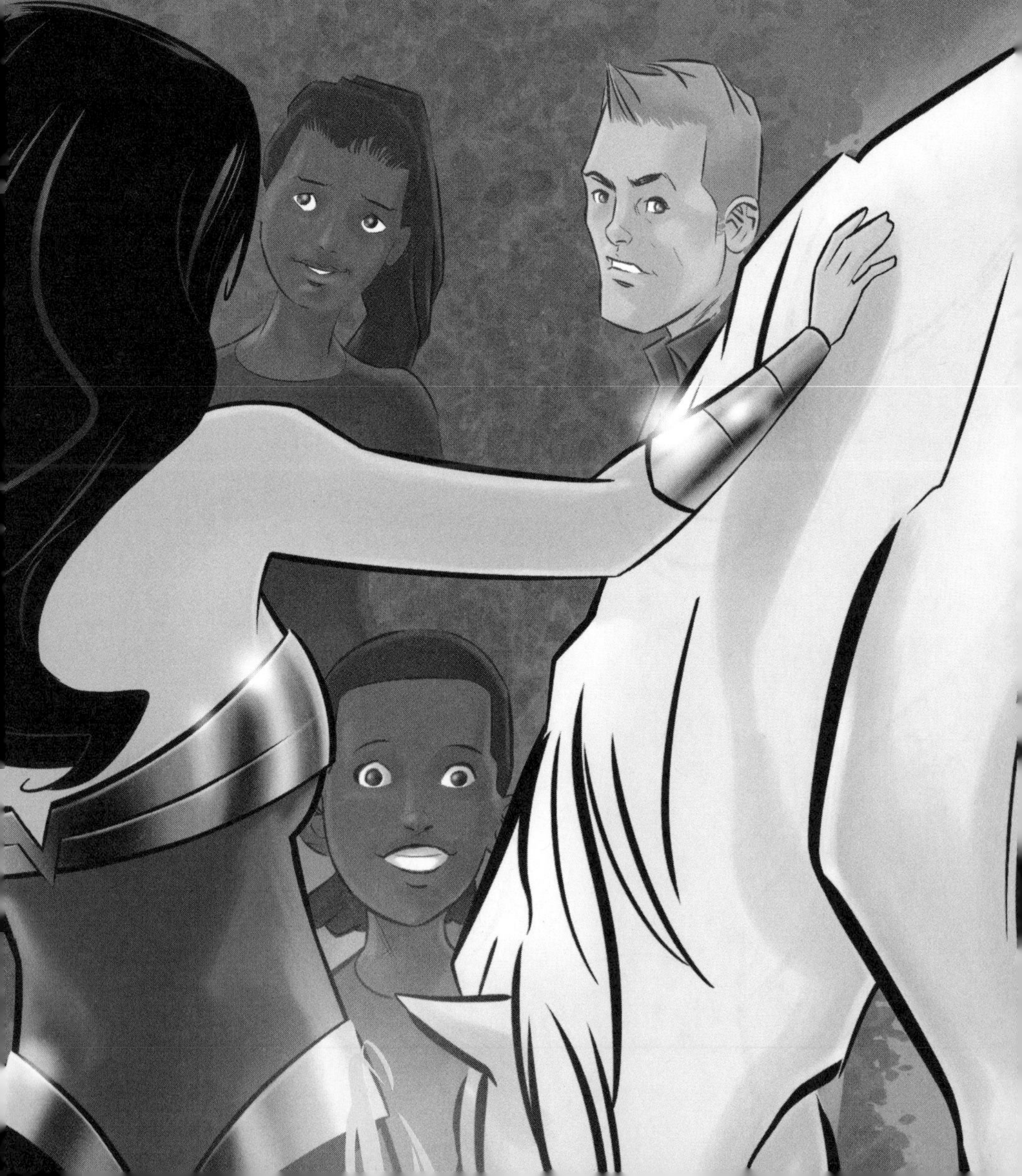

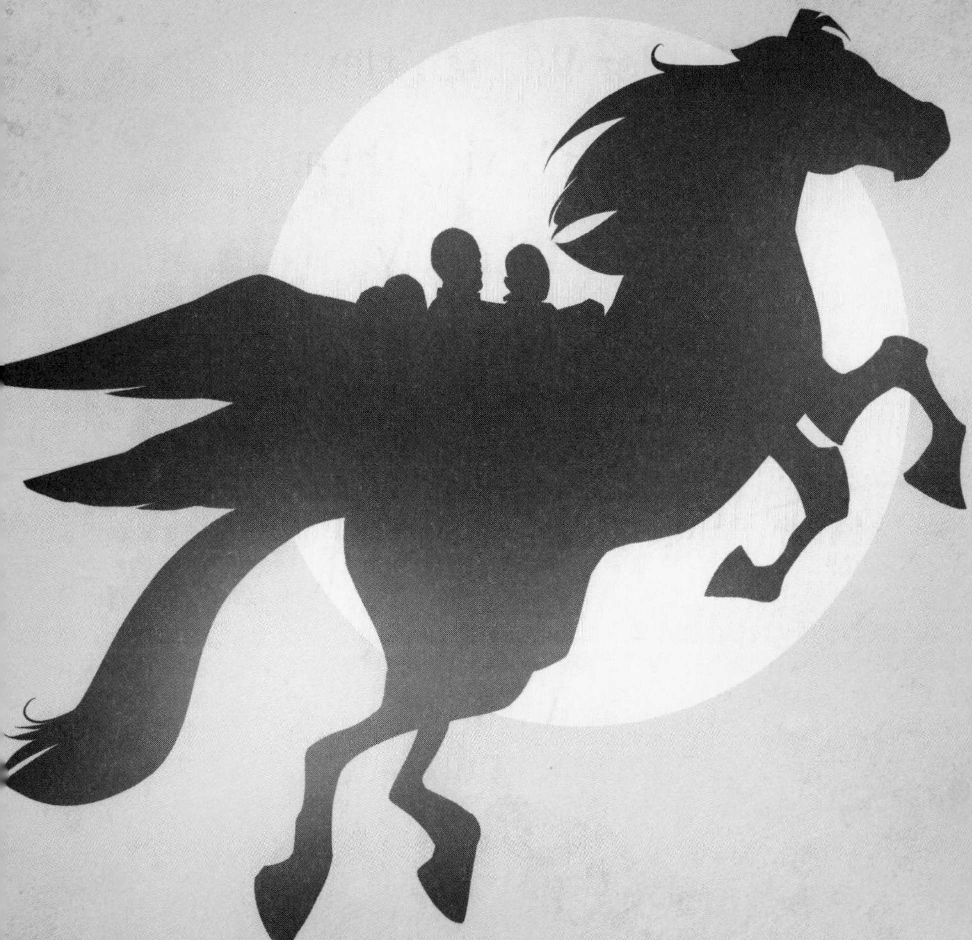

The family climbed
onto the famous winged horse.
Pegasus soared into the air.

Wonder Woman flew
in the air beside them.
She saved the day
and turned Medusa's trap
into a trip to remember!

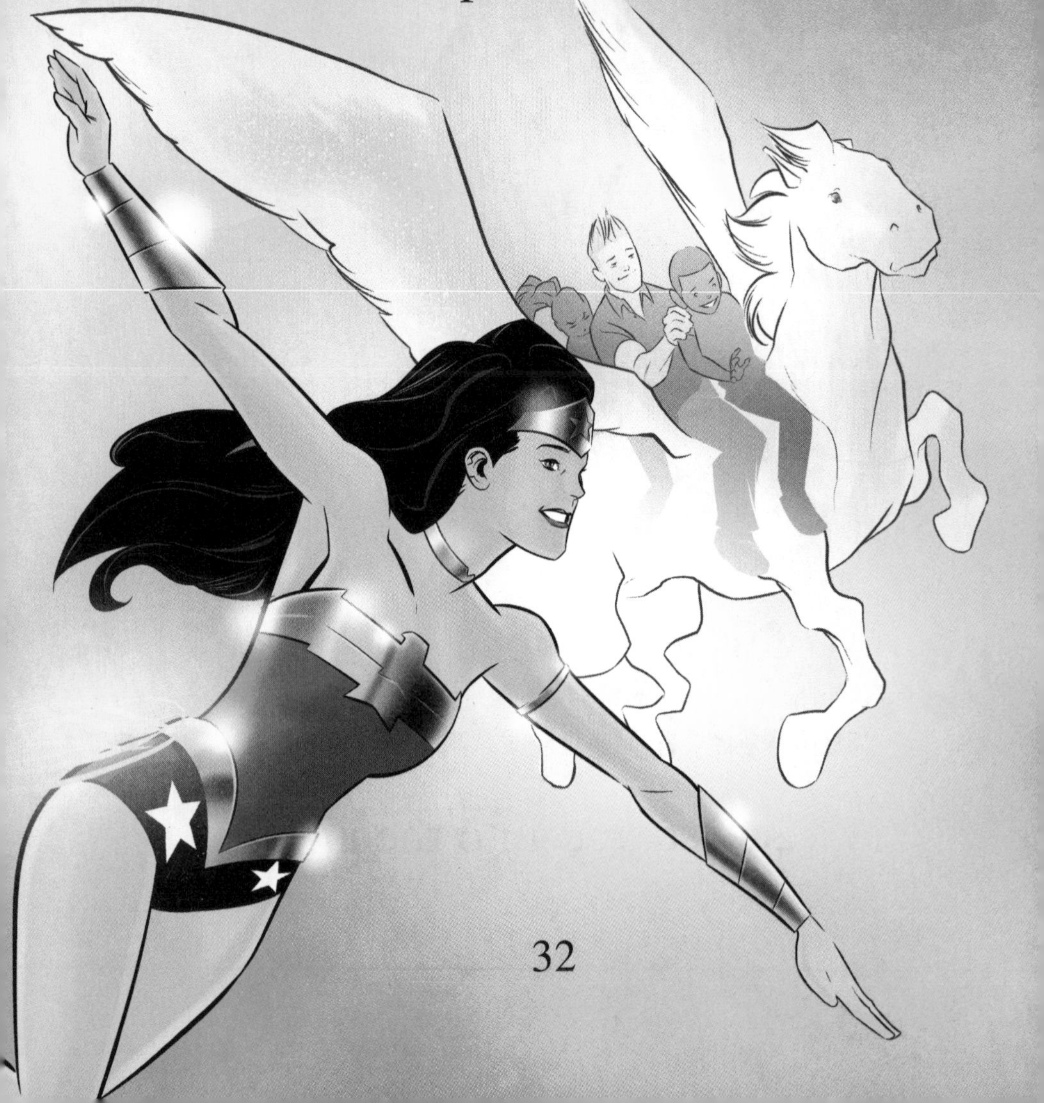